CIARA AND THE LAND OF THE WAVES

奇愛與波浪之土

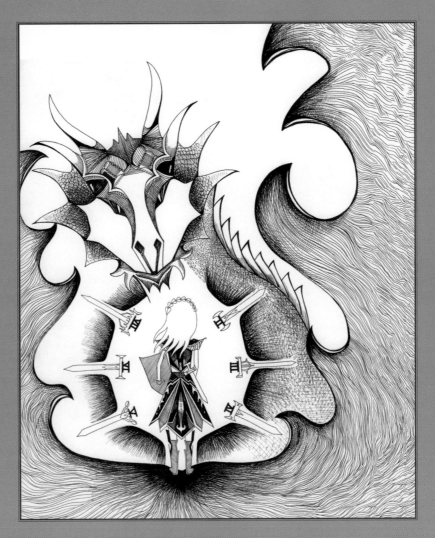

VIVIAN LU

藝術家 Artist Publishing Co.

FOREWORD

Vivian Lu is my niece; her father is the only son of our family. When Vivian came to this world, she received all the blessings and love from both sides of family. I clearly remember when she was born as a premature child. Everyone was very worried about her. It was her mother who devoted her greatest efforts and wisdom with sleepless days and nights to care for her so that Vivian could grow up unblemished, happy, and in good health. Her mother laid the foundation for Vivian to become an outstanding little genius.

Little Vivian had smooth fair skin and always had a sweet smile on her face. She loved to paint from a very early age. She would immerse herself in her paintings as long as she found some free time. Her subjects were full of imaginative spirit. She did not rely on adults' instructions. Soon, her talent won everyone's appreciation; not only did she have many opportunities to show it at school, but she also got a star-like status at home. Her colorful compositions of beautiful paintings were hung from downstairs to the upstairs and new works often replaced the old. Because I was the only member in the family engaged in the arts, I was naturally the one her parents consulted to ask where Vivian could learn art. I strongly opposed sending her to any teachers to learn painting because I noticed her amazing imagination and totally fearless expressions. I feared that if she followed a teacher's guidance, it might ruin her extremely precious gifted nature or limit her original creativities, and that she'd learn to only simulate or echo the visions of aesthetic values in the adult world.

Last year, when Fu Shen and I returned to California, we had a dinner at my brother's house. I saw Vivian not only painted well, but was also particularly capable at telling stories. Each painting was well structured to be published as part of an illustration book, so I encouraged her to develop a specific subject and draw a story book. I also introduced her to Artist Publishing Company. Two months ago, Vivian visited Taiwan with her whole family. She brought the finished work and I was really surprised to see that she could achieve the task of the book so fast during her busy period of study. She started with her concept and drawn from the ideas to the finished point all at once. Not only were her lines very sophisticated, but the plot of the story was also far-reaching, and reminded me of Miyazaki's themes of environmental protection.

Vivian was born and raised in the United States. She created her book "Ciara and the Land of the Waves" with the goal of allowing young readers to participate in the story. She deliberately used black lines to allow the readers to fill in their own colors, and included both Chinese and English to allow them to learn both languages at the same time. Both of these considerations show her mature thoughts towards the significance of the publication and that there is a deeper level of thinking that goes beyond just publishing her artwork. The brave, independent, decisive and curious character of Ciara could be interpreted as her self-projection. I hope this book will inspire children to become more curious about the unknown just like Ciara.

Victoria Lu
Summer 2017 in Los Angeles

序

　　陸欣儀是我的姪女，她的爸爸是我們家的獨子。欣儀來到這個世界時，就收到父母兩邊家庭滿滿的愛。我還清晰記得，她出生時是個早產兒，當年大家都擔心得不得了，完全是她的母親不眠不休用了最大的努力和智慧，讓欣儀絲毫髮未損地快樂健康長大，奠定了欣儀成為一名出色的小天才，母親的努力，是非常重要的基礎條件。

　　皮膚白皙，臉上永遠掛著甜美笑容的小欣儀，從小就喜歡畫畫，只要一有空間，她就會畫圖，題材充滿了想像力，完全不需要大人的指點。很快，她的天份贏得了大家的讚賞，不但學校裡常常給她表現的機會，在家更是獲得明星般的地位，一張張色彩繽紛構圖精美的作品，從樓下一直掛到樓上，經常換檔展出新作。由於我是家裡唯一從事藝術工作的成員，自然被諮詢哪裡去拜師學習，我都激烈反對讓她跟從老師學畫，因為，我看到她驚人的想像力，和完全無畏的表現力，害怕她一旦受到老師的指導甚或限制，就會葬送了她極其珍貴的那種自然天成的原創能力，而只不過去模擬或附和了師長成人世界的審美價值觀。

　　去年，我和傅申回到加州，在弟弟家作客，看到亭亭玉立的欣儀，不但畫畫得好，還特別會說故事，每一幅畫作都非常適合出版成圖文並茂的繪本書，就鼓勵她專門訂一個題目，畫一本故事書，還介紹了藝術家出版社，作為欣儀小朋友奮鬥的目標。兩個月前，欣儀一家回到台灣，帶來了完成的作品，我真的非常驚喜，驚訝她在課業繁忙之餘，還能這麼快達成出書的任務，從構思到完稿一氣呵成，不但繪畫的線條非常老練，而且故事的情節還寓意深遠，頗具宮崎駿環保警世的風範。

　　美國出生長大的欣儀出書，她的《奇愛與波浪之土》，為兒童讀者預設了參與創作的空間，她刻意用白描的手法，讓讀者可以填色，同時，也是一本學習中文或英文的語言教材，顯示出她的思緒成熟，而且對於出版的意義，有更深層次的思考，不只是發表作品而已。勇敢、獨立、果斷和充滿了好奇心的奇愛，好像是欣儀的自我投射，希望這本童書會帶給華文世界的小朋友對未知產生更多的好奇心，就像奇愛那樣。

陸蓉之
2017 年夏天在洛杉磯

PREFACE

A child's imagination is a very special and powerful thing. Dreams, fantasy, and adventure are all core parts of our childhood, our chance to escape into our own worlds. Sometimes, a child's imagination is so powerful that dreams become reality. I sought to capture the whimsy and power of a child's imagination by telling the story of Ciara and her octopus pal Seven as they seek to rescue a town from the flames of Hanba, a dragon drought deity.

Upon opening this book, your first thought may be, why is everything in black and white? That's no fun! Well, I can tell you that it was no mistake. Yes, it was intentional. And for what reason? So that you, as the reader, can fill in the blanks! Add your own colors. Who says that the sky has to be blue and the grass has to be green? As you read this book, you might become a little confused at times because it can be hard to determine whether Ciara is in the real world or within the limitless bounds of her imagination.

Is Seven a real octopus or an imaginary friend? Is Ciara just dreaming? My attempt at creating ambiguity through the use of repeated motifs and dreamlike actions (e.g. a magic locket, flight, randomly appearing armor) is meant to reflect the fine line between a child's imagination and reality. After confronting Hanba, Ciara and Seven are swept up in an ocean wave created by the locket, and the next panel immediately shifts to Ciara's room, where it is morning. Though this may suggest that their journey was in fact a dream, both the puddle next to Ciara's feet and the locket around her neck suggest otherwise…leaving it up to you, the reader, to define what is real. Sadly, I have realized that as children grow up and enter the real world, they often slowly stop dreaming, becoming detached from their imagination and the sense of awe and wonder that accompanies it. I believe that it is important for people of all ages to live life with a sprinkle of magic, and this book serves as a reminder of that. Why is magic important, you ask? Because magic makes life a little brighter.

Finally, I would like to thank everyone who has supported me in the process of creating this book, especially Ms. Marianne Hall for her enthusiasm, encouragement, and mentorship as I continue to develop my artistic vision.

前 言

　　兒童的想像力是非常特別，並且強而有力的。夢想，幻想，以及冒險都是我們童年重要的核心，一個能夠讓我們逃入我們的幻想世界的機會。有時一個兒童的想像力是如此強大，夢想即成為現實。我試圖通過奇愛與小七的故事，講述他們如何從旱魃的火焰，一個龍形的乾旱妖怪手中拯救了村民來捕捉孩子的想像力和奇想的力量。

　　打開這本書您的第一個想法也許是為什麼一切都是黑白的呢？這樣沒有趣啊！我可以告訴您這裡並沒有錯誤。是的，是作者有意如此安排的。但是為什麼呢？所以做為讀者的您可以將空白填滿。加上您自己的色彩。誰說天空一定要是藍色的草地一定要是綠色的呢？當您讀這本書時，有時候您可能會有點困惑，因為可能很難確定到底奇愛是在真實世界裡，或者是在自己無止境的想像力中。

　　究竟小七是真的章魚還是奇愛的幻想朋友？或者奇愛只是在作夢？我嘗試通過使用重複的主題和夢幻般的動作（如魔法項鏈，飛行，隨機出現的裝甲）來創造歧意。這些都是為了反應兒童的想像力與現實之間的細微差別。與旱魃對決之後，奇愛與小七被項鏈所創造的海浪吞食，然後下一頁的圖畫馬上就轉移到早晨奇愛的房間。雖然這可能表明他們的旅程其實只是一個夢境，但是奇愛腳下的一灘水，以及在她脖子上的項鏈提示著或許不是，留給讀者您來定義什麼是真實的。可悲的是，我已經意識到，隨著兒童長大並進入現實世界，他們慢慢地停止夢想，脫離他們的想像力和欽佩的感覺，以及伴隨著的思考。我覺得魔法的火花，對任何年齡層的人的生活是重要的，而這正是本書所要提醒的。或許您會問，為什麼魔法重要呢？因為魔法使生活更明亮。

　　最後，我要感謝所有支持我創作這本書的人，特別是 Marianne Hall 女士，她的熱情、鼓勵和指導，使我能繼續發展我的藝術視野。

On a hot summer's day, Ciara sat crouched at a goldfish scooping stand. Armed with a rice paper net, she tried to catch the tiny goldfish. Splish-nope. Splash-nope. Splash-finally! Wait... an octopus? "Oh well, better than nothing I suppose!" Ciara then headed home.

在一個炎熱的夏日裡，奇愛手拿著紙做的撈網蹲在金魚攤前，水花一次又一次的濺起，但是就是沒有小金魚願意入網。當水花再一次濺起時⋯撈網裡終於⋯等等⋯怎麼是一隻小章魚？「唉呀，有撈到總比沒有好。」奇愛就帶著小章魚回家了。

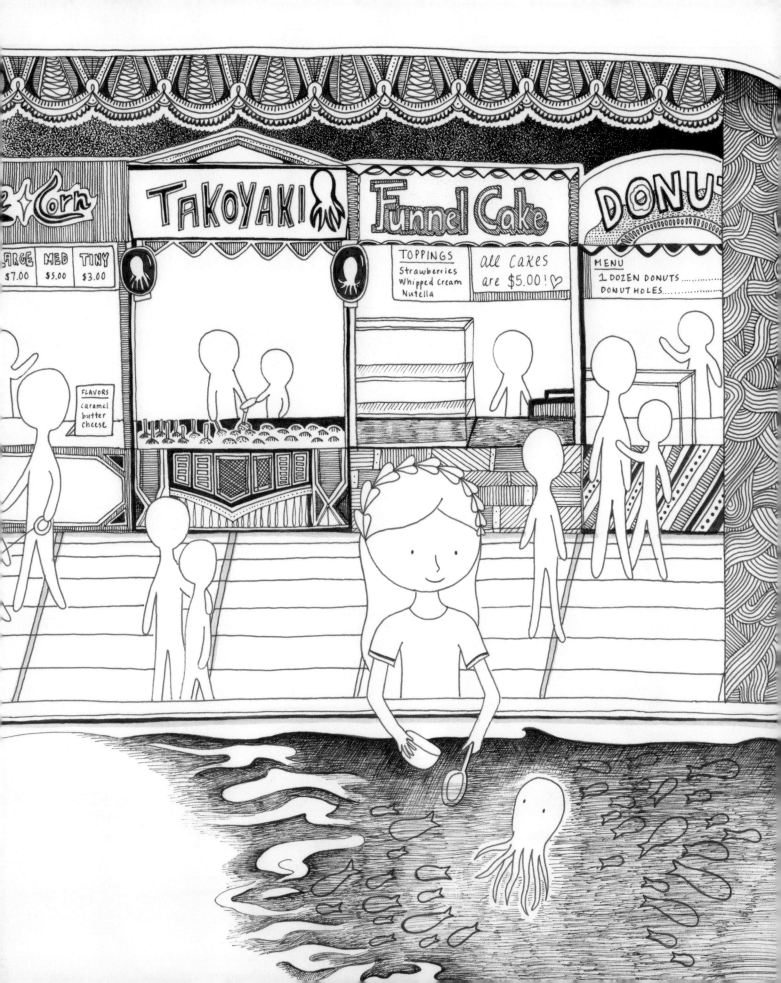

Before going to bed, Ciara placed the octopus in a plastic tub.

睡覺前，奇愛把小章魚放在一個塑膠水盆裡。

That night, Ciara dreamed of a beautiful world. But something was wrong. There wasn't any water, and fireballs were hailing from the sky.

那天晚上，奇愛夢見了一個非常漂亮的世界；但是有些不太對勁，這個美麗的世界裡沒有水，並且還有火球雨正從天而降。

Startled, Ciara woke up from her nightmare. When she opened her eyes, she saw that the octopus she had gotten the previous day was looking at her with a look of distress.

奇愛從惡夢中嚇醒，但是當她張開眼睛的時候，昨天帶回來的小章魚，正愁眉苦臉的望著她。

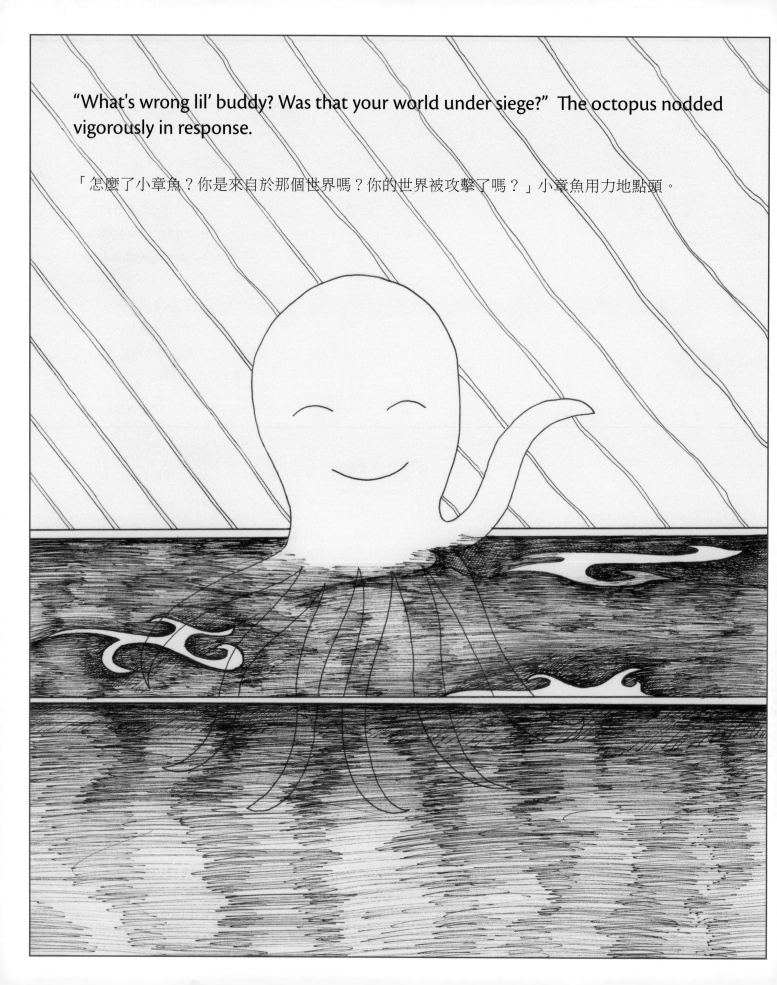

"What's wrong lil' buddy? Was that your world under siege?" The octopus nodded vigorously in response.

「怎麼了小章魚？你是來自於那個世界嗎？你的世界被攻擊了嗎？」小章魚用力地點頭。

"Okay, I'll see how I can help you! But what's your name? What should I call you?
The octopus raised all seven of his tentacles. "Okay, Seven it is then!" The octopus
smiled in agreement.

「好吧，我來想想辦法看看怎麼幫你！但是你叫什麼名字呢？我該叫你什麼好呢？」小章魚舉起
七隻小腳，「嗯，好，就叫你小七！」小章魚笑著點點頭。

Before getting out of bed, Ciara realized that there was a cold lump under her
pillow. A locket!

正準備下床的奇愛，發現在她的枕頭下，有一個冰涼的小項鏈。

As soon as Ciara slipped the locket on, it started floating, guiding her towards the window. Turning around, she glanced at Seven, suspended in a sphere of water and hovering next to her.

當奇愛戴上這項鏈，奇怪的事情發生了，脖子上的項鏈開始飄向窗邊，奇愛轉過身來發現小七正被一團水球包圍著，飄在奇愛的身邊。

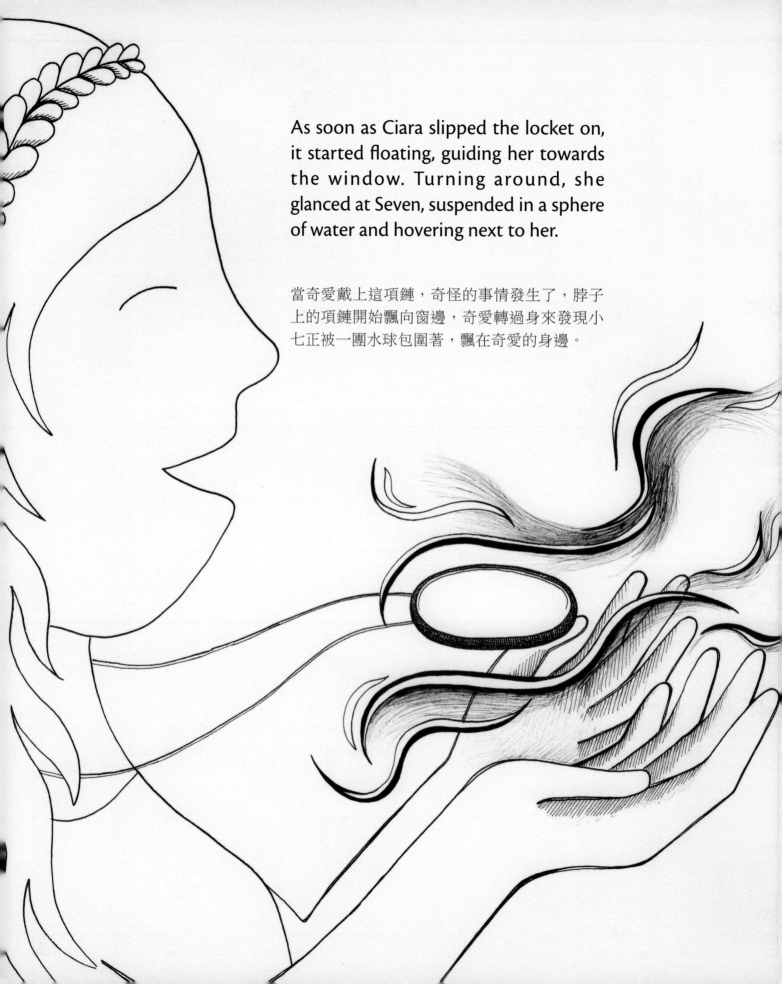

The window opened, and the necklace led Ciara across her hometown as Seven swim – floated next to her. The two glided across urban streets until they reached...

窗子打開了，奇愛脖子上的項鏈，帶著她飛越奇愛居住的小城，小七的水球，也在奇愛的身邊陪伴著她，他們兩個人開始飄過城市的街道，直到他們來到了……

...a cherry blossom path. Numerous lanterns lined the path of pink flowers. When they reached the last tree at the end of the path, Ciara saw that the lantern had a strange shape stamped on the front. The same symbol as her necklace!

一條櫻花道路，有無數的燈籠沿著這鋪滿粉紅花朵的道路。當他們抵達盡頭的最後一棵樹時，奇愛看到在燈籠前面印了一個奇怪的圖案，竟然跟她項鏈上的一模一樣！

Suddenly, a wave of light flashed from the tree, and a gate appeared. The two walked through. Ciara found herself standing in the place she had seen in her dream.

突然間，有一道光芒從樹間射過來，然後出現了一扇門。他們倆走進門裡，奇愛發現自己正站在夢裡看到的地方。

Before Ciara could ask Seven about this world, a lady in a kimono appeared before them.

正當奇愛想詢問小七關於這個世界時，突然一位穿著和服的女士，出現在他們面前。

"I am the gate keeper of this realm, the Land of the Waves. I see you have the Nami locket. You must be a Warrior." The lady had noticed Ciara's locket.

這位女士注視著奇愛身上的項鍊說：「我是這個世界波浪之土的守門人。納米項鍊在妳身上，妳一定是一個戰士」。

"The Nami locket? And what do you mean by Warrior?"

「納米項鍊？戰士？」

The Nami locket is an artifact that allows the wearer to harness the power of the waves and travel between worlds. Whenever the world is in danger, the locket chooses a "Warrior" to protect the realms and keep it safe. It guided you here because it knew our realm was in danger.

納米項鍊是一個神器，它會賦予佩戴者控制水浪的超能力，並且能在不同空間的領域裡來去自如。當一個領域發生危險時，納米項鍊就會選擇一個戰士來保護那個世界。納米項鍊帶你們來這裡，因為它知道我們的世界有危險了。

"As for your octopus pal, he is no ordinary cephalopod. He's your spirit guide and also doubles as your weapon, which you can use in combat. Our world is currently under attack by a huge monster, a yokai named Hanba who has the power to cause droughts. Because of Hanba, people cannot grow food to eat and are losing hope. I know you can unite the townspeople to fight in this battle against Hanba. Your octopus friend will help direct you on your journey."

「你的章魚朋友不是普通的頭足類動物，他是你的精神指導，也是你戰鬥時可以使用的武器。一個巨大的怪物目前正在攻擊我們的世界，這個妖怪叫做旱魃。旱魃有製造乾旱的法力，因為旱魃，人們無法種植糧食來維持生命，並且開始失去希望。我知道妳可以團結鎮民來對抗旱魃的這場戰爭，而妳的章魚朋友也會幫助妳完成使命。」

The petite woman turned back to the two friends. "I wish you all the best luck in the battle against the yokai. If you need anything, feel free to ask."

這個嬌小的女人，轉身面對這兩個朋友：「我祝福妳們能夠成功擊退這個妖怪，如果妳需要任何協助，請儘管告訴我。」

"Thank you very much!"

「非常謝謝妳！」

"No, thank you, Ciara.", the lady replied.

「不，謝謝妳，奇愛。」，穿著和服的女士，笑著回答。

For days, Ciara and Seven traveled
through town, rallying the people
and lifting their spirits as Hanba drew closer.

幾天來，奇愛與小七，他們走過城鎮，聚集了民眾並鼓舞他們的精神，此刻旱魃也越來越接近了。

When Hanba showed up, everyone was ready to fight.

當旱魃出現時，大家都已經準備好要戰鬥了。

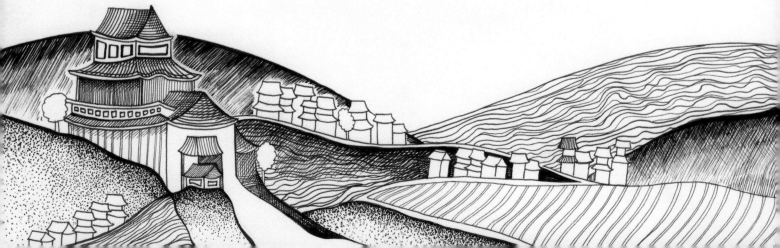

Holding up the Nami locket, Ciara cheered alongside the townspeople, "We will fight as one! Hanba, you will cease to exist from this earth!"

舉起納米項鏈，奇愛和鎮民們一起歡呼：「我們將團結一致戰鬥，旱魃，你將從地球上消失！」

Everyone started to charge. The archers fired their arrows, the farmers ran with their pitchforks, and the soldiers slashed with swords.

大家開始進攻，弓箭手射出他們的箭，農夫們拿起他們的草叉向前衝，而士兵們舉起他們的刀劍往前砍。

In the mist of all the chaos, the Nami locket started to glow, surrounding Ciara and Seven. The ocean's waves suddenly rose and circled the monster – trapping it inside. As the yokai struggled inside the water, Seven transformed into seven dancing blades and slayed the creature.

在一片混亂之中，納米項鏈開始發光，它的光芒圍繞著奇愛與小七。這時候海洋的波浪，突然升起圍住了怪物，把它關在裡面。正當妖怪在水浪中掙扎的時候，小七突然變成七把刀劍，刺死了妖怪。

However, as the ocean's waves pulled back, Ciara and Seven were dragged into the vortex of water. Spinning in the water, Ciara didn't know what to say. She simply had too many thoughts running through her mind. As the water surrounded them both, Ciara could hear the townspeople chanting, "Thank you, Ciara and Seven! Water has returned to our world! We will no longer be stricken by droughts!"

然而，隨著海洋波浪的退去，奇愛與小七也被捲入水中。奇愛在水中旋轉著，不知道該說什麼，她的腦海中浮現了太多想要問的問題了。當海浪圍繞著他們倆的時候，奇愛聽見人們歡呼著說，「謝謝妳，奇愛與小七！水已經回到我們的世界了！我們不再被乾旱襲擊了！」

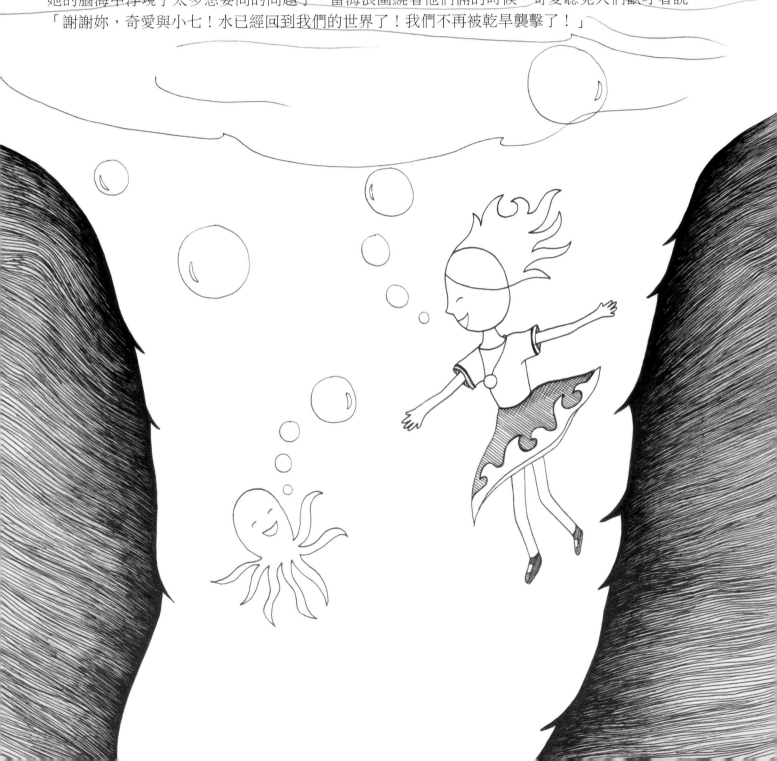

In awe, the townspeople watched the water envelop the two heroes. As they watched the waves recede, they ran to see if the girl and octopus were still there, but they were gone. Two cherry blossoms laid in their wake.

人們敬畏地看著水包圍著兩位英雄，直到海浪退走。鎮民們急忙跑去看看女孩跟章魚是否還在，但是她們已經不見了，留在那裡的，只剩下兩朵櫻花。

Ciara found herself in her room, with Seven at her side. It was now morning. The Nami locket was around her neck, and everything in her room was exactly as it had been before they'd left – that is, beside the puddle of water surrounding her feet. Exhausted, Ciara looked at Seven, content in his bubble of water.

奇愛發現自己回到了房間裡，小七也在身邊，而且已經是上午了。納米項鏈還在奇愛的脖子上，房間裡的一切都和她們離開前一模一樣，除了奇愛腳下有一小潭水。疲倦的奇愛，看了看小七，小七滿足安穩的睡在它的水泡中。

Ciara wondered about the Land of the Waves. What would happen now that Hanba was gone? What about the lady in the kimono who had helped them? She decided that she would one day return to the Land of the Waves to find out, but as her stomach grumbled in distress, she realized that there were more pressing matters at hand...

like breakfast!

奇愛心中想著波浪之土，不知道旱魃消失之後現在怎麼樣了？還有那個穿著和服曾經幫助過她們的那位女士？奇愛心中決定有朝一日一定要再回到波浪之土。這時奇愛的肚子突然咕嚕咕嚕地叫著，於是奇愛確定這時候更緊迫的事情是…先吃頓早飯吧！

CIARA AND THE LAND OF THE WAVES
奇愛與波浪之土

Vivian Lu（陸欣儀） 著

發 行 人　何政廣
主　　編　王庭玫
編　　輯　洪婉馨
美　　編　張娟如
出 版 者　藝術家出版社 Artist Publishing Co.
　　　　　台北市金山南路（藝術家路）二段165號6樓
　　　　　TEL：(02) 2388-6715・2388-6716　FAX：(02) 2396-5708
　　　　　6F., No. 165, Sec. 2, Jinshan S. Rd.(Artist Rd.), Taipei 106, Taiwan
　　　　　Tel: 886-2-23886715. 23886716　Fax:886-2-23965708
　　　　　E-mail: artvenue@seed.net.tw　www.artist-magazine.com

郵政劃撥　50035145 藝術家出版社帳戶

總 經 銷　時報文化出版企業股份有限公司
　　　　　桃園縣龜山鄉萬壽路二段351號
　　　　　TEL：(02) 2306-6842
南區代理　台南市西門路一段223巷10弄26號
　　　　　TEL：(06) 261-7268
　　　　　FAX：(06) 263-7698

製版印刷　鴻展印刷股份有限公司
初　　版　2017年9月
定　　價　新臺幣280元
I S B N　978-968-282-203-6（精裝）